Cable Cars

by Lola M. Schaefer

Consultant:
Sharon Phelan, Assistant Manager
Cable Car Museum
San Francisco, California

Bridgestone Books
an imprint of Capstone Press
Mankato, Minnesota

Bridgestone Books are published by Capstone Press
818 North Willow Street, Mankato, Minnesota 56001
http://www.capstone-press.com

Copyright © 2000 Capstone Press. All rights reserved.
No part of this book may be reproduced without written permission from the publisher.
The publisher takes no responsibility for the use of any of the materials
or methods described in this book, nor for the products thereof.
Printed in the United States of America.

Library of Congress Cataloging-in-Publication Data
Schaefer, Lola M., 1950–
Cable cars/by Lola M. Schaefer.
  p. cm.—(The transportation library)
  Includes bibliographical references and index.
  Summary: Discusses the invention, development, and operation of cable cars, particularly in the United States.
  ISBN 0-7368-0361-0
  1. Railroads, Cable—Juvenile literature. 2. Street-railroads—Juvenile literature. [1. Cable cars (Streetcars)] I. Title. II. Series.
TF148.S33 2000
625.5—dc21   99-20215
                                                                                                          CIP

Editorial Credits
Karen L. Daas and Blanche R. Bolland, editors; Timothy Halldin, cover designer and illustrator; Heather Kindseth, illustrator; Kimberly Danger, photo researcher

Photo Credits
Archive Photos, 12–13
Corbis, 14, 16–17
Ed Kashi, 6, 8 (inset)
Index Stock Imagery, cover
James P. Rowan, 18
John Elk III, 4
Root Resources/James Blank, 8–9, 20

Table of Contents

Cable Cars 5

Traveling by Cable Car 7

Parts of a Cable Car 9

How a Cable Car Works 11

Before the Cable Car 13

The Inventor of the Cable Car 15

Early Cable Cars 17

Cable Cars around the World. 19

Cable Car Facts 21

Hands On: How A Cable Car Grip Works 22

Words to Know 23

Read More 24

Internet Sites 24

Index. 24

Cable Cars

Cable cars are vehicles that travel on tracks in streets. Steel cables under streets move the cable cars. Cable cars carry passengers on city streets. Today, San Francisco, California, is the only city that has cable cars.

vehicle
something that carries people or goods from one place to another

Traveling by Cable Car

People buy tickets to ride cable cars. Cable cars pick up passengers at cable car stops. Conductors take the passengers' tickets. Passengers sit or stand on cable cars. Different cable cars travel on different routes.

route
the path a vehicle or person takes to get from one place to another

Parts of a Cable Car

Cable cars have several main parts. Passengers sit on a cable car's seats or stand and hold onto poles. A gripman pulls a grip lever. This joins the grip to a cable. The long cable lies under the ground between the tracks. A cable car has three brakes.

> **grip**
> a device that grabs an object; a cable car grip grabs a cable that moves the car forward.

brake
grip
lever
brake
cable
brake
grip

cable
engine
Powerhouse

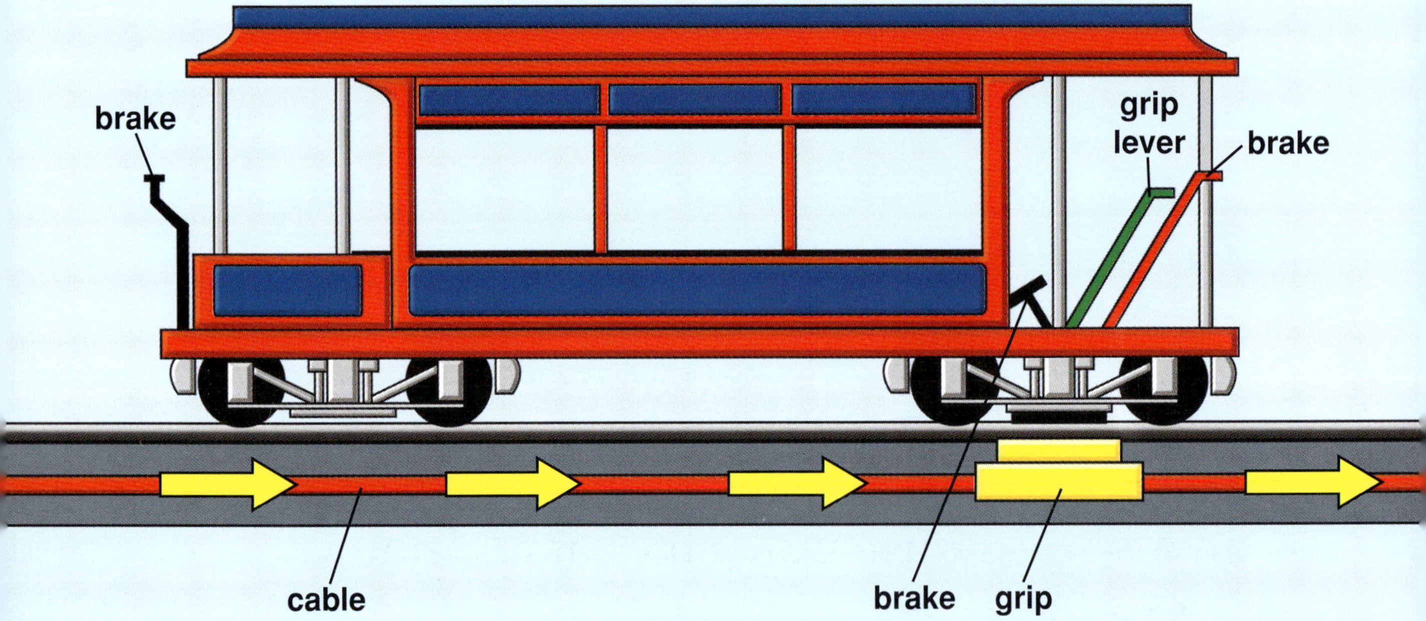

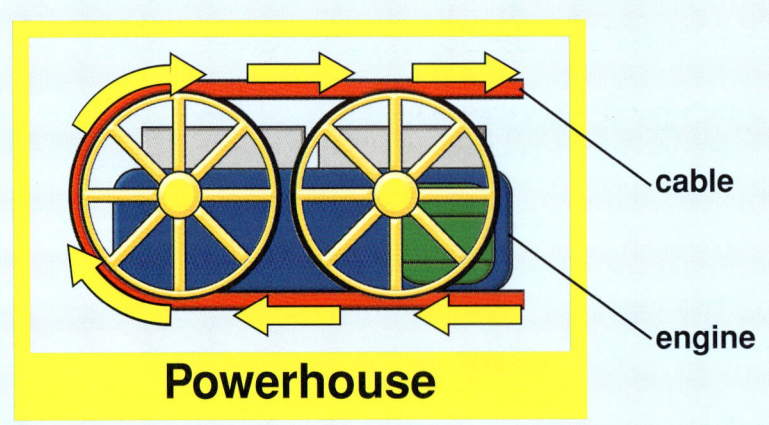

How a Cable Car Works

A gripman pulls a grip lever to join the grip to the cable. Electric engines in a powerhouse move the cable. The cable car moves forward when the grip grabs the cable. The gripman uses brakes to stop the cable car and to control its speed.

Before the Cable Car

People in cities traveled mainly by horse before cable cars were invented. Horses pulled some railway cars along tracks on city streets. But horses could not pull cars up steep hills. Horses slipped and sometimes caused accidents.

The Inventor of the Cable Car

In 1873, Andrew Hallidie invented the cable car in San Francisco. Andrew saw a street car accident. A car pulled by four horses slid down a steep hill. Andrew owned a company that made cable. He realized that cable could make street cars safer.

Early Cable Cars

Early cable cars had more than one car. The front car towed passenger cars. A gripman rode in the front car. He worked the grip lever and brakes. Steam engines in a powerhouse moved the cable.

Cable Cars around the World

Many cities had cable cars in the late 1800s. Trolley cars then became popular. Trolley cars were cheaper to use than cable cars. But cable cars worked better on steep hills. Cities in Australia, New Zealand, and Scotland had cable cars until the mid-1900s.

trolley
an electric streetcar that runs on tracks; overhead electric wires power trolleys

Cable Car Facts

- Cable cars only move forward. Gripmen push the cars around on a turntable at the end of each route.

- One cable car weighs about 12,000 pounds (5,443 kilograms).

- The steel cables must be replaced every 110 to 230 days.

- San Francisco cable cars carry about 13.5 million passengers each year.

- The first cable car carried 90 passengers up a steep hill in San Francisco.

- The first cable car outside of San Francisco ran in Dunedin, New Zealand.

Hands On: How A Cable Car Grip Works

A moving cable pulls cable cars. Gripmen loosen the grip to slow down or stop a cable car. But the cable keeps moving. You can see how this works using clothesline and a clothespin.

What You Need

5 feet (1.5 meters) clothesline
two friends
table
spring clothespin

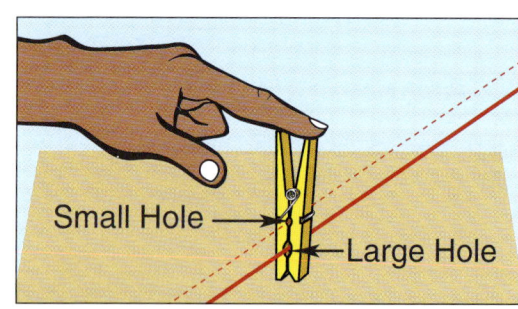

What You Do

1. Have two people each hold one end of the clothesline about 1/2 inch (1.2 centimeters) above the table.
2. Clip the clothespin so that the clothesline goes through the large hole of the clothespin. The clothesline is like the cable. The clothespin is like a grip in a loose position on a cable car.
3. Hold the clothespin upright by placing a finger flat against the top.
4. Have one person pull the clothesline. The cable car does not move forward when the grip is loose.
5. Clip the clothespin to the clothesline using the small hole. The clothespin is like a grip in a tight position on a cable car.
6. Repeat steps 3 and 4. The cable car moves when the grip is tight.

Words to Know

grip (GRIP)—a device that grabs an object; a cable car grip grabs a cable that moves the car forward.

gripman (GRIP-man)—a person who operates the grip lever on a cable car

inventor (in-VENT-or)—a person who thinks of and makes something new

passenger (PASS-uhn-jur)—someone other than the driver who travels in a vehicle

powerhouse (POW-ur-houss)—part of a cable car system; a powerhouse is a building that holds engines that move cables.

Read More

Badt, Karin Luisa. *Let's Go.* A World of Difference. Chicago: Children's Press, 1995.

Barrett, Norman. *Transport Machines.* Visual Guides. New York: Franklin Watts, 1994.

Burton, Virginia Lee. *Maybelle, the Cable Car.* Boston: Houghton Mifflin, 1996.

Internet Sites

The Cable Car Home Page
http://www.geocities.com/CapeCanaveral/Launchpad/3518/cablecar.html

Cable Car Inventor—Andrew Hallidie
http://www.sfmuseum.org/bio/hallidie.html

San Francisco Cable Cars
http://www.sfcablecar.com

Index

cable, 5, 9, 11, 15, 17, 21
conductors, 7
gripman, 9, 11, 17, 21
Hallidie, Andrew, 15
horses, 13, 15
passengers, 5, 7, 9, 21

powerhouse, 11, 17
routes, 7
San Francisco, 5, 15, 21
tracks, 5, 9, 13
trolley cars, 19
turntable, 21